Little Chef

Adapted by Natasha Bouchard

Illustrated by Barbara Nelson, Ron Husband, and John Raymond

Designed by Disney Publishing's Global Design Group

Inspired by the art and character designs created by Pixar

A GOLDEN BOOK · NEW YORK

Copyright © 2007 Disney Enterprises, Inc./Pixar. All rights reserved. Published in the United States by Golden Books, an imprint of Random House Children's Books, a division of Random House, Inc., New York, and in Canada by Random House of Canada Limited, Toronto, in conjunction with Disney Enterprises, Inc. Golden Books, A Golden Book, and the G colophon are registered trademarks of Random House, Inc.

ISBN: 978-0-7364-2447-9

www.randomhouse.com/kids/disney

Printed in the United States of America
10 9 8 7 6 5 4 3 2 1

Remy is a rat with an important job. He's in charge of smelling the garbage to make sure it's safe to eat.

Remy does not like garbage, but his brother
Emile will eat anything!

The rats live in an attic, and Remy knows that the best food is downstairs. But Remy's dad, Django, warns him, "Stay out of the kitchen and away from humans."

But Remy can't resist going into the kitchen. He loves good food and even dreams of becoming a chef.

Remy finds a piece of cheese in Emile's bag. He thinks it would taste great with a mushroom he found.

Remy cooks the mushroom and the cheese together over the chimney. The plan goes well until—*crack*—lightning strikes!

The bolt of lightning melts the cheese on the mushroom perfectly!

Remy thinks his meal needs a spice. He and Emile
sneak inside to the kitchen to look for it.

Emile doesn't think being in the kitchen is a good idea.
He knows it's a dangerous place for rats.

Remy shows Emile his favorite cookbook,
written by Auguste Gusteau. Emile can't believe
that Remy can read!

A TV show explains that Gusteau was a famous French chef who once owned a popular restaurant in Paris.

The old woman who lives in the house wakes up
from her nap and finds Remy and Emile.
She doesn't like rats.

The ceiling falls in, and all Remy's friends and family tumble down from the attic.

The rats must escape.

But Remy can't leave without Gusteau's cookbook!

The rest of the rats climb onto rafts and escape,
leaving Remy behind.

Remy tries to catch up to his family,
but they're moving too fast.

Remy goes for a wild ride on the rapids.

Remy is sad, lonely, and very hungry.
He hopes his family will find him soon.

Suddenly, Remy finds himself talking to Gusteau!
Or is it Remy's imagination?

Gusteau tells Remy to go aboveground and look for food. Remy runs through the sewer pipes in search of something to eat.

Remy finally finds some bread, but before he can enjoy a bite, Gusteau visits him again. Gusteau reminds Remy that he is a cook, not a thief.

Remy keeps searching. He discovers he's in Paris, at Gusteau's famous restaurant! He can't believe his eyes.

Inside Gusteau's restaurant, the kitchen is very busy.
Everybody has a special job to do.

Linguini is hired to take out the garbage and wash dishes. He gives a letter to Skinner, who doesn't like him.

Remy looks down into Gusteau's restaurant through
a skylight on the roof. He's excited to see
a real gourmet kitchen in action!

Linguini is a klutz and accidentally spills some soup!

Remy watches Linguini try to fix the soup.
But Linguini is really making it worse!

Suddenly, Remy falls through the skylight
and splashes into the kitchen sink.

Remy runs for safety. Cooks don't like rats
in the kitchen.

Remy runs past Linguini's soup and then stops.
He knows he can fix it. This is his chance
to cook in a real kitchen.

Remy is so busy that he doesn't notice Linguini staring at him. Linguini has never seen a rat cook before.

Skinner sees Linguini by the soup pot and thinks Linguini was cooking the soup. "How dare you cook in my kitchen?" Skinner shouts at him.

"Stop that soup!" Skinner cries out to the waiter.
But the waiter is gone and it is too late!

The soup is served . . . and the customer loves it!
Colette also thinks it's delicious!

An angry Skinner tells Linguini that he must make the soup again or he'll be fired. Suddenly, Skinner sees Remy! Linguini catches Remy, and Skinner orders him to get rid of the rat.

Linguini has an idea. Maybe Remy can make the soup!
So instead of getting rid of Remy, Linguini
asks for his help.

Remy agrees to help Linguini.

The next morning, Linguini wakes up to find Remy cooking breakfast. Linguini is amazed by this little chef.

At the restaurant, Linguini hides Remy in
his jacket before going inside.

Remy tries to control Linguini's movements
by crawling around under his jacket. This makes
Linguini scream and jump.

Remy is hungry. Linguini feeds Remy some cheese
and hopes he won't get into trouble.

Skinner suddenly marches in. Did he see a rat?

Remy discovers that he can move Linguini like a puppet by pulling on his hair. This works much better than crawling under Linguini's clothes!

Later that night, Linguini and Remy
practice cooking together.

It works! Linguini is able to make the soup again!
Skinner can't believe it.

Skinner has Colette teach Linguini to cook.
She's the toughest cook in the kitchen, and she
tells Linguini to keep his station clean.

Linguini thanks Colette for teaching him how to cook. He likes her . . . and she's beginning to like him, too.

Skinner finally reads the letter Linguini gave him. It says that Linguini is Gusteau's son, but Linguini doesn't know! Skinner fears he will have to give the restaurant to Linguini if the young man finds out.

Skinner has a trick up his sleeve. He gives Linguini a recipe he knows will taste bad so that Linguini will fail. Then Skinner can fire him.

At the last minute, Remy makes Linguini change the recipe so that it will taste better.

Mustafa announces that the customers love the dish!
Skinner's trick didn't work. Skinner thinks Linguini
is hiding something.

Skinner thinks he's seen a rat. He tries to get
Linguini to tell him what is in his hat.

Meanwhile, Remy finds Emile behind the restaurant.
Remy wants to give his brother some good food to eat.

Remy is gathering up some cheese for Emile when Gusteau appears again. Gusteau reminds Remy that he shouldn't steal, but Remy says it's just this once.

Emile thinks this is the best "garbage" he's ever eaten,
but Remy tells him to keep it a secret.

Emile takes Remy to where his family has been living in the sewers underneath Paris.

They celebrate Remy's return with a party!

Remy tells his dad that he has a new life in Paris and cannot stay with the family.

Remy says that he's been working with humans.
Django can't believe his ears! He asks Remy
to follow him.

Django shows Remy that humans
can be very dangerous to rats.

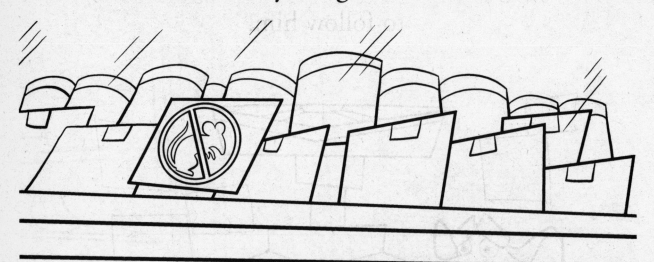

The next morning, Remy finds Linguini asleep
on the restaurant's kitchen floor!

When Colette arrives, she wonders why Linguini is ignoring her. She does not know that Linguini is asleep and Remy is controlling Linguini's moves.

Linguini finally wakes up and tries to explain
why he's been acting so strange.

Remy is worried that Linguini will reveal their secret.
He must stop Linguini, so he pulls Linguini's hair.

Linguini's lips land on Colette's, and they kiss!

The news spreads across Paris that Gusteau's restaurant is again *the* place to eat. The famous food critic Ego wonders why.

Skinner does not want Linguini to become
a famous chef or the owner of the restaurant.
He wants to get rid of Linguini! But how?

Colette takes Linguini on a motorcycle ride.
But poor Remy can't hold on. She's going too fast!

Back at the restaurant, Remy finds
Emile and his friends. They ask Remy for food.

Remy looks in Skinner's office for the key to the walk-in refrigerator. Gusteau appears again and reminds Remy not to take food from the restaurant.

While in the office, Remy discovers that Linguini is Gusteau's son and the real owner of the restaurant!

Skinner finds Remy reading the papers and chases him.

Skinner must get the papers back, or the secret that Linguini is Gusteau's son will be revealed! But Skinner isn't fast enough to catch Remy.

With Remy's help, Linguini finds out that he's the true owner of Gusteau's. He fires Skinner. The restaurant becomes popular again, and everyone wants to meet Linguini!

Ego warns Linguini to be prepared. Tomorrow night,
he will review the restaurant.

Remy thinks Linguini spends too much time with reporters when he should be working on their cooking.

Skinner sees Linguini and Remy arguing. At last, he understands—a rat is helping Linguini cook!

Remy doesn't like the way Linguini is acting.
Maybe his dad was right about humans. Remy leads
his family to the walk-in refrigerator to take
all the food they want.

When Linguini finally goes back to the restaurant to tell Remy that he's sorry, he catches Remy stealing food. He orders Remy to leave and never come back.

The next day, Remy tries to save Emile from a trap but gets caught instead!

The trap was set by Skinner! He doesn't want Remy to help Linguini cook for Ego.

The time has come! Ego arrives to review the restaurant.

The kitchen is in an uproar. Linguini doesn't know what to do without Remy.

Meanwhile, Remy's family saves him from Skinner's trap. Remy then dashes back to the restaurant to help Linguini get a good review from Ego.

Linguini tells Remy that he's sorry, and he tells the other cooks all about him. The cooks can't believe it, and they walk out. They will not cook with a rat.

Django is proud of Remy for being so brave, and he thinks Linguini might not be a dangerous human after all. He gets all the rats to help in the kitchen.

But Skinner won't give up. He calls the
health inspector to shut down the restaurant!
Quickly, the rats go after the inspector!

Colette has a change of heart and goes back to the restaurant. She decides to help Remy and his friends.

Ego is served ratatouille as the main course.

Skinner is surprised to find the kitchen swarming with rats! Remy's friends capture Skinner so that their secret will be safe.

Ego asks to meet the chef.

Ego loves the dish! He gives the restaurant a good review, but the health inspector closes it down.

Remy goes on to make his dream come true!
He opens a restaurant with Linguini and Colette
where he can cook delicious food.

The restaurant is small, but it welcomes everyone who loves good food! And its special dish is ratatouille.